WITHDRAWN

A YEAR WITH
MAMA EARTH

For Magdalene
—Rebecca Grabill

For Lori
—Rebecca Green

A YEAR WITH
MAMA EARTH

Written by
Rebecca Grabill

Illustrated by
Rebecca Green

Eerdmans Books for Young Readers
Grand Rapids, Michigan

Mama Earth rustles her autumn wings
to cool her hot, tired face.
She sighs, and the first September frost
crackles over bowing stalks of corn.
Pumpkins peek out from under
wide, yellowing leaves.
They've been playing peek-a-boo,
shaded from the blistering heat
all this time.

Carved and lit from within,
October's pumpkins grin.
Mama laughs a chill wind
that stirs the maple leaves
into a golden whirl
while children spin and spin,
their scarves like twirling maple seeds,
until they tumble in a laughing heap.

November's stubborn oak holds tight
to her curling, crinkly leaves.
Mama Earth sings
a lullaby to the fat black bear,
the round woodchuck,
the woolly caterpillar,
the infant wrapped in blankets,
while the busy squirrel packs
the last few nuts
into his summer stores.

In December, Mama Earth dons
her winter coat, white and soft,
trimmed with crimson berries.
She sings the song of cardinals
that peck up pumpkin seeds
scattered on the snow.
She dresses holly shrubs in icicles
and thanks her children
for long strings of cranberries
left on the evergreens.

In January, the white world won't hear
of warming up. No,
Mama sends all warmth south
to find the geese and ask
if they're enjoying their vacation.
Silent deer grow brave in January,
and Mama Earth loads the trees' arms
with white, and blows light fluff
against the windowpane.

By February, even the sparrows shiver,
heads together, wings tucked tight.
Rabbits spring over snow
that wears ice like a shell,
while the deer's feet sink deep,
each step crackling with Mama Earth's
soft smiles. She whispers for spring
to wake the sleeping crocus.
And deep, deep beneath the winter coverlet,
spring breathes one long, expectant yawn.

In March, Mama Earth leaves a layer of mud
beneath the snow to dress the snowman on the lawn.
Oaks give up the last of autumn's leaves.
The sugar maples sing a sweet song
of pancakes swimming in amber syrup.
The doe tiptoes
across Mama's damp carpet
with last spring's fawn,
and they shed their winter coats
of foggy gray for soft spring brown.

In a breath of pink and white,
the dogwood, redbud, apple cry,
"It's time! It's time!"
and Mama Earth's sunny smile cracks
the last of April's ice along the river's
edge. Her children float
their paper boats and dream
of Ferris wheels and cotton candy
pink and soft as the branches
thick with buds above their heads.

May perfumes Mama Earth with violet
and honeysuckle. Ferns unfurl their lacy arms
to greet Mama's gentle friend, the sun.
And seedlings in the garden
push out their first prickly leaves,
ripe with the promise
of fat melons and late
summer squash.

In June, dizzy bees roll
in open blooms until their bodies
turn yellow with summer's sugar.
Mama Earth sends the laughing brook
to young deer for splashing,
to raccoons for rinsing their paws,
and to children, to tease them into slipping
off their shoes and socks
to join the fun.

July brings dancing rain,
and fireflies, and crickets
that sing till morning.
Mama tightens night's reins
and lets day play and play and play
until the bats give up on waiting.
They dine on mosquitoes
while children toast marshmallows
over a crackling fire.

By August, her children have soaked the sun
straight into their bones,
and still Mama Earth bakes the ground
dry as toast. The peeper frogs
hide until dewy evening
before coming out to sing their joy.
Mama Earth shares carrots and turnips
with the rabbits, and the pumpkins
again play their silly games beneath
wide green leaves.

Soon it's September again.
Mama Earth drives night
into evening, faster, faster, faster.
The squirrel pauses her work
only long enough to wave
goodbye to geese traveling
to their winter home.
Mama Earth waters her parched ground,
making puddles for eager boots.
She gathers icy diamonds in her skirt,
saving them. She will cast them
across the grass some night soon,
when she sighs out
fall's first glistening frost.

author's note

A Year with Mama Earth began as a reflection, a celebration of my most-beloved memories of childhood, memories I wanted to share with my own children. Walks in the woods, everyday moments of wonder that changed with each season. Intricate Queen Anne's lace, a stream-polished pebble of quartz, deer tracks in the snow. I still love the way each season sings—with its own voice—a melody anyone who listens can hear. The rush of the summer stream, the delicate *ffp ffp ffp* of falling snow. Who is the singer? A gentle, fun-loving mother full of surprises and care for all her creatures!

To write this book, I moved beyond my childhood memories to more current explorations, like pumpkins and corn grown in the garden—things I didn't experience as a child in urban Muskegon, Michigan. I also absorbed the work of creators I love, like writer Annie Dillard and photographer Dewitt Jones, and I spent joyful hours in the woods looking, listening, inhaling. I researched to answer my own questions: what is the creature actually called, the one I grew up knowing as the tree toad? It's a spring peeper frog, whose song I still hear from the marsh down the hill from my house three seasons out of four (not just spring).

Now nature is the backdrop to my year. It's my calendar, my clock. I know the school bus will soon arrive when the trees along the driveway separate from one gray mass into individual trunks. I know autumn is just around the bend when the tiger lilies along the road droop and their green leaves take on a tinge of chartreuse. The language of stillness can only be heard in stillness, stillness of mind and heart.

No matter where we are, the world is speaking to us. In the woods, the city. Try it.

Stop. Listen.

Let your ears hear all the sounds. Then pick out one sound and hear that only. Open your eyes and see. It's the lesson of the earth, to hear the whisper of a voice as small and still as a raindrop rippling a puddle at your feet.

— Rebecca Grabill

illustrator's note

Illustrating *A Year with Mama Earth* brought back wonderful memories for
me, as I grew up in Michigan where each month is unique and promising.
From September's warm pumpkin patches to February's icy blue wind,
I was inspired both by Rebecca's words and by my
own personal experiences. The characters were
developed to portray the personal relationships
we share with one another during the seasons,
and how we also relate to nature throughout
the changing months.

While some of the illustrations were drawn from
memory, I also did further research to learn about the
plants and animals in the story. Did you know, for instance,
that there are three generations of monarch butterflies born
in one year in Michigan? For May's illustration, I drew a beautiful
yellow butterfly, which would be from the second generation,
usually born in May and June. I also studied peeper frogs,
woolly caterpillars, maple syrup production, and
spring crocuses.

My favorite things to draw, though, were the squirrels.
In Michigan the squirrels are large, round, and brown.
Do you have squirrels where you live? What do they
look like?

— Rebecca Green

Text © 2019 Rebecca Grabill
Illustrations © 2019 Rebecca Green

Published in 2019 by Eerdmans Books for Young Readers,
an imprint of Wm. B. Eerdmans Publishing Co.
Grand Rapids, Michigan

www.eerdmans.com/youngreaders

Manufactured in China

27 26 25 24 23 22 21 20 19   1 2 3 4 5 6 7 8 9

ISBN: 978-0-8028-5505-3

A catalog record of this book is available from the Library of Congress.

Illustrations created digitally.